Hyperion Books for Children ▲ New York

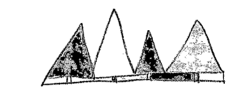

LITTLE TREE

poem by e. e. cummings

story and paintings by chris raschka

little tree
little silent Christmas tree
you are so little
you are more like a flower

who found you in the green forest
and were you very sorry to come away?
See   i will comfort you
because you smell so sweetly

i will kiss your cool bark
and hug you safe and tight
just as your mother would,
only don't be afraid

look   the spangles
that sleep all the year in a dark box
dreaming of being taken out and allowed to shine,
the balls the chains red and gold the fluffy threads,

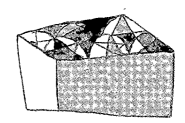

put up your little arms
and i'll give them all to you to hold
every finger shall have its ring
and there won't be a single place dark or unhappy

then when you're quite dressed
you'll stand in the window for everyone to see
and how they'll stare!
oh but you'll be very proud

and my little sister and i will take hands
and looking up at our beautiful tree
we'll dance and sing
"Noel Noel"

—e. e. cummings

The little tree had a little dream. The little tree dreamed of being a Christmas tree, a beautiful Christmas tree in a city, far, far away in a place he'd never seen but only dreamed of, with his own little family in his own little house.

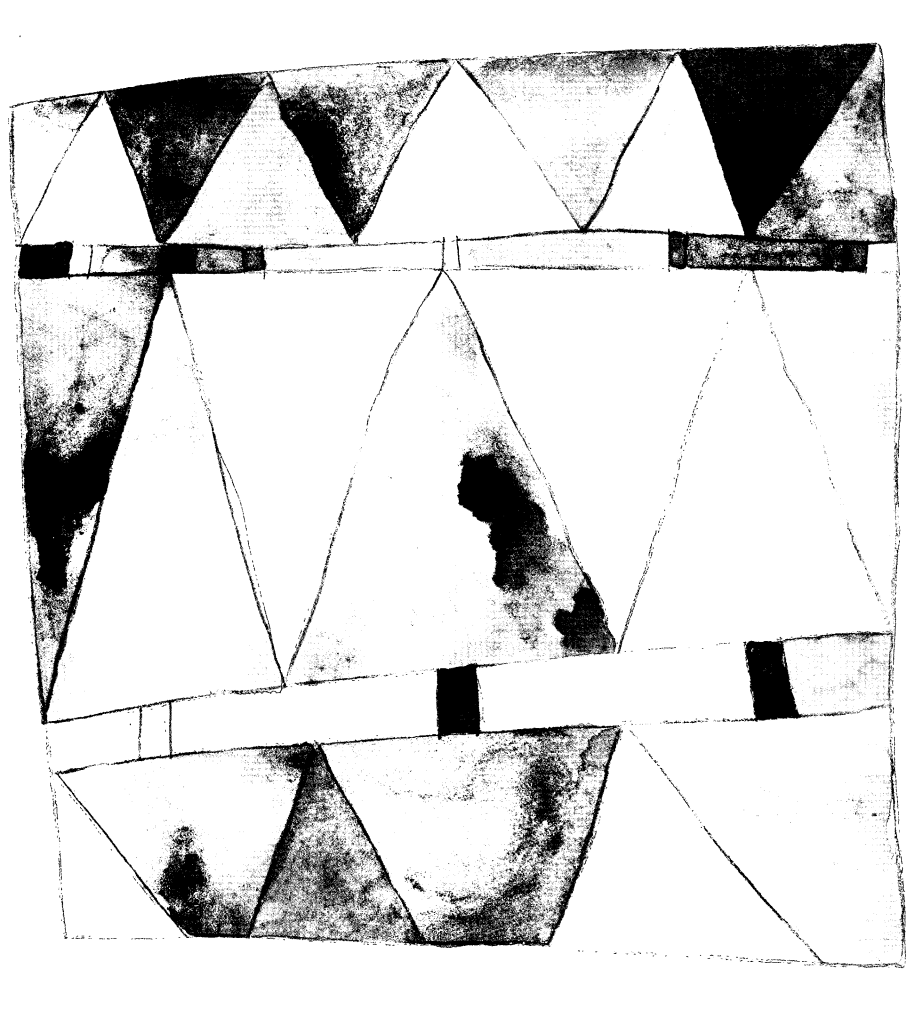

The little tree had to leave the little green forest,
the mountains, and all the other trees he had known
all his little life, to find a new life, his dream life,
in a far, far away place.

A little truck drove back and back, back and back into the mountains and found the little tree standing on his little hill.

The little truck
took the little tree
to a little train.
The little train
rolled through
the mountains,
over the hills,

past the farms
and little towns
to the little big city.

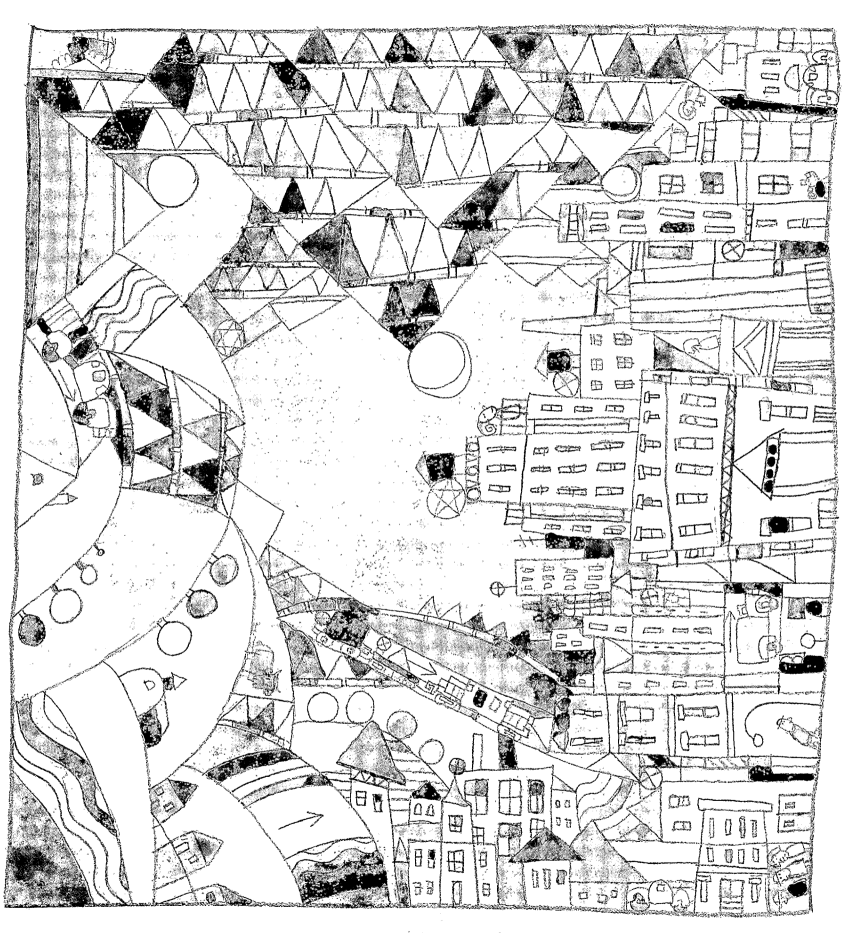

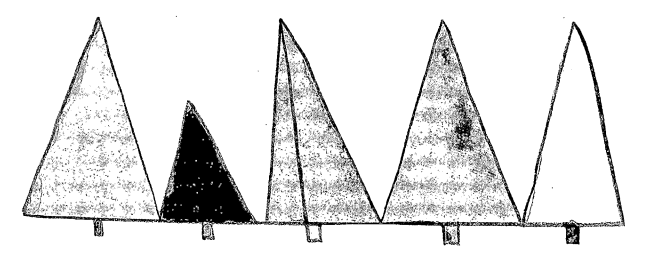

The little tree stood
with the other trees
on a little sidewalk
on a little street in
the little big city.

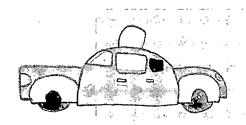

A little boy, a little
girl, a little mother
and father and their
little dog walked
up and down the
little streets of
the little big city,
looking and looking
for their own
special, just right,
one and only,
perfect little tree.

At last they found the little tree,
their own little tree, waiting for them
on the little sidewalk.

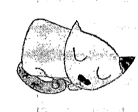

The little family
hailed a cab and
took their little
tree to their little
apartment building.
The little doorman
lifted the little tree
out of the trunk.
The little elevator
carried the little family
and the little tree up, up, up
to the little family's little home.

The little girl and the little boy decorated the little tree.  The little tree lifted up his little branches, like little arms, to show off all the little ornaments, ribbons, chains, and lights. The ornaments had come from other far away places just to hang in the branches of the little tree. The little dog barked at the little blinking lights.

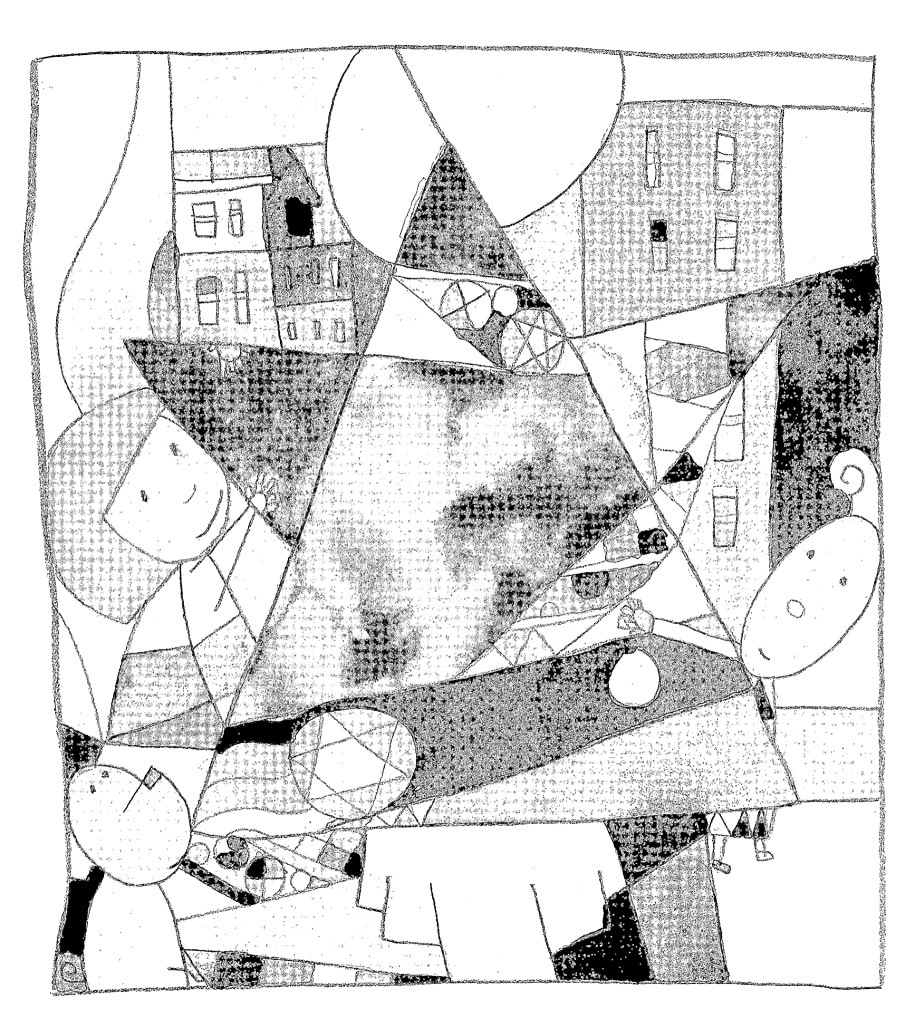

The little tree had found
  his own special place in the world,
    a special little place that was
      waiting for him all his life.

For Ken

Printed in the United States of America
First Edition
1 2 3 4 5 6 7 8 9 10

This book is set in 15-point Deepdene

Library of Congress Cataloging-in-Publication Data
Cummings, E. E. (Edward Estlin), 1894–1962.
Little tree / poem by E. E. Cummings ; story and paintings by Chris Raschka.— 1st ed.
p. cm.
Summary: Inspired by a poem by E. E. Cummings, this is the story of a little tree
that finds its own special place in the world as a much-loved Christmas tree.
ISBN 0-7868-0795-4 (trade)
1. Christmas trees—Juvenile poetry. 2. Children's poetry, American.
[1. Christmas trees — Poetry. 2. American poetry.] I. Raschka, Christopher, ill. II. Title.
PS3505.U334 L5 2001
811'.52—dc21 2001016631

Visit www.hyperionchildrensbooks.com

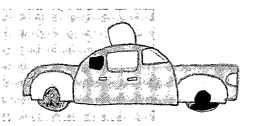

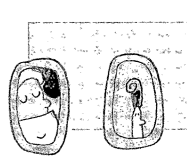